3-MINUTE
SLEEPYTIME STORIES

Good Nights

We all want bedtimes to be peaceful and happy, leading to quiet sleep for little ones – and for the grown-ups who love them! Sometimes, the events of the day, whether happy or troubling, are not so easily put to rest. These stories aim to make the transition between busy days and calm nights easier.

A story can be a lovely part of a bedtime routine, but some stories are not very soothing. The stories in 3-*Minute Sleepytime Stories* have been written specifically for this special time. They are very short — no page-turning needed — but give lots of opportunities for talking together, so that grown-ups have a chance to discover any anxieties and offer reassurance, and little ones can be encouraged to share their feelings, whatever they may be.

Each story touches on a different issue of the kind that sooner or later affects almost every child. Look at the index of themes on page 80 to choose a story that relates to what is happening in your lives. It is easy just to skim through yourself first to make sure it is what you both need.

Wishing you good nights and happy days …   *NMAB*

3-MINUTE
SLEEPYTIME STORIES

Written by Nicola Baxter

Illustrated by Pauline Siewert

ARMADILLO

Wishing special sweet dreams to
Nathan, Ashley and Lewis

This edition is published by Armadillo, an imprint of Anness Publishing Ltd,
Blaby Road, Wigston, Leicestershire LE18 4SE; info@anness.com

www.annesspublishing.com

If you like the images in this book and would like to investigate using them for publishing,
promotions or advertising, please visit our website www.practicalpictures.com
for more information.

Publisher: Joanna Lorenz
Editor: Elizabeth Young
Text: Nicola Baxter
Illustrations: Pauline Siewert
Designer: Amy Barton
Editorial Consultant: Ronne Randall
Production Controller: Wendy Lawson

A CIP catalogue record for this book is available from the British Library.

PUBLISHER'S NOTE
The author and publishers have made every effort to ensure that this book is safe
for its intended use, and cannot accept any legal responsibility or liability for any
harm or injury arising from misuse.

Manufacturer: Anness Publishing Ltd, Blaby Road, Wigston,
Leicestershire LE18 4SE, England
For Product Tracking go to: www.annesspublishing.com/tracking
Batch: 6542-21585-1127

Contents

Twitchety Toes

There once was a boy with twitchety toes,
Two fidgety knees, an itchety nose.
He couldn't, wouldn't snooze or doze.
Did he *ever* sleep, do you suppose?

There once was a boy with a busy head,
Who tossed and turned all over his bed.
"I'm thinking too hard to sleep," he said.
Do you think he stayed awake instead?

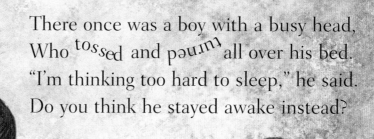

There once was a boy whose ears were wiggly.
His eyes were bright. His voice was giggly.
His squirming made the bedspread jiggly.
Did *you* ever know a boy so wriggly?

6

If ever you feel you have twitchety toes,
Or fidgety knees, or an itchety nose,
If ever you find your head is busy,
Your thoughts are whirly and twirly and dizzy,
If ever your ears begin to wiggle,
If ever your voice begins to giggle,
Or squirming makes your bedspread jiggle,
Then you should know, it's *good* to wriggle.

Yes, wriggle your feet and wiggle your toes,
Jiggle your legs and your arms and your nose,
Then str-e-e-e-tch your body from bottom to top,
And str-e-e-e-tch again, then s-l-o-w-l-y stop.

Let all your toes go floppy and still,
Relax your legs and your arms until
All of you starts to feel heavy as lead,
Sinking into your snuggly bed.

And as your eyes begin to close,
You'll forget that you ever had twitchety toes.

7

Recipe for a Dream

You will need:
a snuggly bed
a special grown-up
lots of love
some big cuddles

a kiss or two
a cuddly toy (optional)
a bedtime story
(this one will do nicely)
a sleepy little person

Method:

1. The special grown-up should put the sleepy little person into the snuggly bed. The sleepy little person may need to check that it is the right bed. Mistakes can happen when grown-ups are tired or busy.

2. The sleepy little person should give the special grown-up lots of cuddles and some kisses. Grown-ups like this.

3. The sleepy little person must persuade the grown-up to go away. Sometimes grown-ups take ages to say good night, and it is very, very difficult to get started on a dream when they are around.

4. The sleepy little person should lie still with eyes closed and just let all the funny, silly, lovely, strange things inside his or her head come floating by. If anything scary turns up, just push it away gently. There is plenty of other stuff. Sooner or later, some of those funny, silly, lovely, strange things will stop floating past and turn into a fantastic dream.

5. What do you mean, there's nothing in your head? I bet there are ice cream cones and elephants, trucks and sunflowers, superheroes and mermaids, princesses and pizzas, big shiny boots and birthday cakes. Aren't there? Of course! That's plenty for a perfect dream.

What? That grown-up is still there?
You know what to do. Say good night quickly
and kindly … and start dreaming!

9

Grrrumfffgggrf!

One night Joe came downstairs and told his mother he had something very important to say to her. And he had to say it **now**.

"It would be better if you told me in the morning, Joe," replied his mother, looking at the clock.

Joe shook his head.
"It's serious," he said firmly.

"All right," sighed his mother.

Joe came closer and spoke in a low voice. "There's a monster in my bedroom," he said.

"Again?" asked his mother.

Now it was Joe's turn to sigh. "Those other monsters," he said, "were *real*, but they were inside-my-head monsters. This one is an out-there monster."

"What does it look like?"

"I haven't *seen* it," said Joe. "I've *heard* it."

"OK," his mother replied. "What does it sound like?"

"It goes like this," whispered Joe.

Grrrumfffggggrf!

Joe's mother almost dropped her coffee mug, but she was smiling. "Joe," she said, "that was an excellent monster noise. I know exactly what that monster is like. Come with me."

On her way, she whispered something to Dad.

Upstairs, the two monster-hunters sat on Joe's bed. "Ssshh," whispered the bigger one. "Any minute now we'll hear it."

Grrrumfffggggrf!

Dad rushed in at the sound. "You were right," he said. "It's the Greater Gushing Flush Gurgler. A very annoying monster. We'll definitely have to call that plumber back."

Then Joe knew exactly what the monster was. It wasn't scary at all. Do you know, too?

11

The Perfect Bed

Rebecca was a lovely child
But still she drove her parents wild.
She wouldn't stay in her own bed.
"I can't *sleep* like this!" her father said.

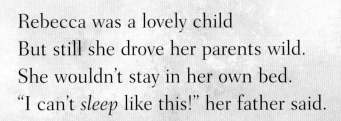

Rebecca's mother had a plan.
She went to see Rebecca's gran.
"Well, I'm not sure," her granny said,
"But I will help you change her bed."

Soon Becky had a huge surprise.
She said, "I can't believe my eyes!"
Her bed was gone. There was instead
A gorgeous, curtained, princess bed.

"I'll never leave it," Becky smiled.
Her parents hugged their pretty child.
But still they woke when tiny toes
Kicked Dad rudely on the nose!

Becky's dad told Becky's gran,
Who said, "Now we will try *my* plan."
That night when Becky went to bed,
She found her sister there instead.

"I think *she'll* love this princess bed,
And *you* don't sleep here," Mother said.
"You can sleep with Dad and me,
Although there's not *much* room for three."

Rebecca went away to think.
Her princess bed was white and pink,
And really it did not seem fair
To see her little sister there.

So in the middle of that night,
Her parents saw a lovely sight,
When into Becky's room they crept,
There was their princess . . . and she slept.

13

Lots of Love

Daytimes are busy times. They are filled with doing and seeing, and talking and playing. Sometimes there is a little bit of shouting and stamping, too. But bedtimes are great times for thinking and remembering . . .

all the people you love best in the world

the clothes you like most

your very best friend

the toys you love to play with

a song you love to sing

the games you love to play

things you love to eat and drink

the stories you love to hear again and again

and how warm and snuggly your little bed feels tonight.

How lucky you are to have so many people to love and so many wonderful things to do. And the special person who is reading this to you feels lucky, too, you know. Because that special person loves . . . *you!*

The Busy Night

O ne night, when it was time to go
to sleep, Annie said, "No, wait!"

"What is it, Annie?" said someone who loved her more
than the moon and stars. "You need to go to sleep now."

"How long is it until morning?" Annie asked.

"It's about eleven hours until you wake
up," said the person who loved her more
than sunshine and flowers.

"That," said Annie, "is a very, very long
time. I don't want to go to sleep. Nothing
will happen for *eleven* hours!"

"Nothing will happen?" cried the person
who loved her more than comfy slippers
and cakes. "The world we live on will be
turning. And all the little animals and
birds that come out at night will be

scurrying and hurrying. And big trucks will be rumbling through the dark. And lots of people will be busy all night long getting everything ready for another day . . . and for *you*!"

"That's a lot of busyness," said Annie slowly. It made her feel tired to think of it.

"The good news," said the person who loved her more than smiles and chocolate, "is that you don't have to do any of it. All you have to do is lie here, all snuggly and warm, and go to . . ."

But Annie had guessed what she had to do.
She was already busy . . . sleeping!

17

The Wobbly Tooth

One day Clara looked in the mirror and let out a yell. It was like this:

Waaaaaagggggahhhhhhhhahhhahhahhhhhah!

Her mother came running. "Sweetheart! What is it?"

Clara wailed some more. "Look!" she yelled. She put her finger in her mouth and poked. One little tooth at the bottom was wobbly.

"Wow!" said her mother. "What a big girl you are now! Your grown-up teeth are getting ready to grow, so it is time for your baby teeth to come out."

"Waaaaaahhhhh!" shouted Clara. She put her hand over her mouth. "All at once?"

18

"No, no. One by one," her mother smiled. "It's not a bad or scary thing, Clara. It's great. And when a tooth comes out, the tooth fairy might bring you a surprise."

Clara liked the idea of that. She cheered up enough to forget all about her tooth for at least five minutes.

Then she said, "What if the tooth fairy can't find me?"

"The tooth fairy is magic," replied her mother. "She can always find you."

Clara whispered her biggest worry. "What if I *swallow* it?"

"The tooth fairy will know even if you do. But I'm sure you won't. Teeth usually fall out when you're awake."

Days went by. The tooth got wobblier and wobblier and wobblier. It fell out while Clara was playing, but her mother wrapped it up in a tissue and brought it home so Clara could put it under her pillow that night. And what do you think happened then?

19

Growly Grandpa

Bobby was staying with his granny for the first time. He loved being with her. But when Grandpa came in at suppertime, Bobby wasn't so happy. He didn't like the way Grandpa growled.

"Supper will just be a minute," said Granny.

"Hmmmph," said Grandpa, but because he was a bear, it sounded more like "Grrrrrrmph!"

"Had a busy day?" asked Granny.

"Grrrrrrrmph!" said Grandpa, picking up the newspaper. Granny noticed that Bobby was hiding, but he was too frightened to come out. Grandpa was such a very big, very grumpy, very growly old bear.

Granny sat down with Bobby in her lap. He buried his face in her cuddly, furry arms.

"You know," said Granny to Grandpa, "inside this scared little bear is a very brave and clever little bear."

"Grrrrrrrmph!"said Grandpa.

"You know," said Granny to Bobby, "inside that growly, grumpy big bear is a very kind and smiley big bear."

Bobby looked at Grandpa doubtfully. Grandpa looked at Bobby.

"Grrrrrrrmph!" said Grandpa, but Bobby saw that his eyes were smiling.

"Grrrrrrrmph!" said Bobby, though he wasn't at all as growly as Grandpa.

Then Grandpa laughed a deep, growly laugh, and Bobby laughed, too. Soon he was sitting on Grandpa's knee and looking at the newspaper with a very kind and smiley big bear, who was every bit as cuddly and furry as Granny.

Much Too Loud!

*T*here was once a little girl who could **not** fall asleep. She wanted to. She really did. But she couldn't.

So the little girl got out of her bed and went to the top of the stairs. She called out as loudly as she could. Then someone who loved her very much came running upstairs to see what was the matter.

"Why are you out of your bed?" the someone gently asked.

"I can't sleep," said the little girl. "The TV is much too loud."

"Let's go into your room and listen," said the someone who loved her. "This is a serious matter."

So the little girl got back into her bed and listened hard and said, "See? I can still hear it, and it is stopping me from going to sleep."

The someone who loved her listened hard, too. "You know," said the someone, "that is really a very soft sound. I don't think it is the noise of the TV that is keeping you awake. I wonder if you think you are missing out on something interesting downstairs."

"Maybe," said the little girl. "Am I?"

"No way!" said the someone who loved her. "It is a very boring TV show. I am nearly falling asleep myself. But do you know what that very soft TV sound means? It means that the people who love you best in the world are right there, just downstairs, and you are safe and sound in your snuggly bed. And that very soft sound means it is OK for you to go to sleep with a smile on your face just like the one I see now."

So the little girl smiled and closed her eyes. The someone who loved her smiled and slipped away. And soft sleepy sounds filled the peaceful house.

Busy, Busy Baby

*T*alking about the day that has passed is a great way of getting ready to sleep. This poem gives prompts for conversations between the verses. It is easy to adapt for your own day.

Oh, busy, busy baby,
What have you done today?
Can you remember how today began?
Busy baby, what do you say?

Oh, busy, busy baby,
What have you done today?
What did you have for breakfast?
Busy baby, can you say?

Oh, busy, busy baby,
What have you done today?
When you got dressed, what did you wear?
Busy baby, what do you say?

Oh, busy, busy baby,
What have you done today?
This morning, what did you do and see?
Busy baby, what will you say?

Oh, busy, busy baby,
What have you done today?
What did you love to eat for lunch?
Busy baby, please do say!

Oh, busy, busy baby,
What have you done today?
Tell me about your afternoon!
Busy baby, what can you say?

Oh, busy, busy baby,
What have you done today?
What did you eat at suppertime?
Busy baby, what do you say?

Oh, busy, busy baby,
What have you done today?
Who helped you to snuggle in your bed?
Busy baby, what do you say?

Oh, busy, busy baby,
You have done so much today!
You must be so, so sleepy.
"Good night!" is what we say.

Are You There?

Billy had a big worry. It was so big, he didn't **want** to think about it. It was so big, he really **couldn't** talk about it. But each day, the worry got bigger and bigger and bigger…

One night, when the person Billy loved best in all the world was tucking him into bed, the worry got so big it just burst out of him.

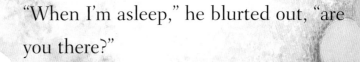

"When I'm asleep," he blurted out, "are you there?"

"Am I where, sweetheart?" said the person who loved him best in the world, too. She was folding his clothes.

"Are you there?" shouted Billy. "Are you in the house, downstairs or somewhere? Or do you (here came the big worry) go away?"

"Go away?" said the clothes-folder and tucker-inner. She came to sit down on the side of his bed.

"I would never, ever, ever leave you alone!" she said, in a very serious voice. "When you are asleep, you are always being loved and looked after. Always. Sometimes, just sometimes," she went on with a little smile, "I do go out for the evening. Then I always, always find someone nice to stay with you. I am very, very, **very** careful about who I choose."

Then she hugged him and whispered in his ear. "You see, worries nearly always go away, but I never, ever will."

*Then Billy felt a warm, fizzy, happy feeling, and it was bigger than the worry had **ever** been!*

Home

Toowoo, who was a big owl, and Lulu, who was a medium-sized owl, and Oona, who was a baby owl, lived in a hole in a tree. They were warm, and snug, and happy.

One day, when the owls were sleeping, a big wind came blowing by. Leaves and twigs and little branches swirled past. The owls, snuggled up in their tree-trunk home, cuddled close to each other.

Then they heard a **creeeeaak!**

And a **craaaaaack!**

And a **horrible craaaaash!**

Their tree slo-o-o-w-w-w-ly toppled over onto the ground.

28

The owls picked themselves up and fluttered their feathers. "Everyone all right?" asked Toowoo.

"Just fine," hooted Lulu.

"Ooooooo!" moaned Oona.

She wasn't hurt at all, but she was very upset.

"We'll wait until the wind takes a rest," said Lulu. "Then we'll find ourselves a lovely new place to live."

"Nooooo!" cried Oona.

Toowoo and Lulu wrapped Oona up in their big, soft wings and told her something important.

"It isn't a tree trunk," said Toowoo, "that makes a home. It's a family. Wherever there are owls who love each other living together, that is home. And it is a perfect home."

So that night, the owls flew off together and found just the right place. They cuddled together inside. And suddenly, a strange new place *was* home. And it was **perfect**.

The Baby Present

One day, Jordan's mother sat down beside him and gave him a cuddle. "I've got some exciting news," she said.

Jordan looked up. "A real bike? A TV in my room? A puppy?"

His mother laughed. "No! Better than any of those! In a few weeks, you're going to have a little sister. Won't that be lovely?"

"Lovely," said Jordan quietly.

He knew a little bit about babies because his friend Josh had a new brother. Josh's brother cried a lot. Josh had to keep quiet when his brother was sleeping. Josh's mother and father were sometimes too tired to play with him.

Jordan wasn't sure he wanted a baby sister. When his mother patted her tummy and smiled, he knew she was thinking about the baby. She wasn't thinking about *him*.

Jordan was very quiet for the rest of the day. That night, his dad came up to his room to say good night.

"You know, Jordy," he said, "when you were born, I was a bit worried. I loved your mother so much I didn't think I'd have any love left for you. But you know what? When you came, you brought the love with you. And I love you more and more each day. I think your sister will be the same. There'll be *plenty* of love to go around."

Dad was right. Jordan's little sister came with pink cheeks, and wispy hair, and little hands that curled around his fingers, and so much love that Jordan felt warm all over.

When you were a baby, you brought sooooo much love with you, too.
And you know what?
You still do!

Ally Gets Angry

Ally was playing with her toy rabbit one evening when the person she loved best in the world came to tell her it was time for bed.

"No!" shouted Ally. "I don't want to go! I'm playing with Harry!"

"Ally, you sound angry," said the person she loved best. "You know it is bedtime now. So come along."

"I *am* angry!" Ally yelled. "And I'm *not* coming!" And to show how angry she was, she pulled Harry's ear so hard it came off!

Ally looked down at poor Harry. She sat down on the floor and burst into tears.

The grown-up who always loved Ally—even when she was angry—sat down beside her and said, "Oh, Ally, you have got big feelings inside you. It is hard, isn't it, when your feelings are so strong? Let's think about what you can do next time you have big, difficult feelings."

They tried
taking big, deep breaths
and letting the feelings
whooosh out.

They tried
stretching up high, high, high
and letting the feelings
flow out of their fingertips.

They tried
putting their hands
on their hips
and saying loudly,
"Oh skibbledibble!"

Ally now knew what to do when she felt angry.
She went to bed
with a happy smile.
And later, when the grown-up
had fixed him up,
so did Harry!

33

Bedtime Story

Here is a story that you can tell all by yourself! (Or you could ask the person who tucks you in to help, if you like.) Start at Bedtime Island and travel wherever you like, saying what happens. Make sure you get back to Bedtime Island before you go to sleep!

Start from Bedtime Island.

Set sail in a submarine!

Visit the fizzing volcano!

Have fun with the happy octopus!

Meet mermaids here!

Discover the Smiling Isles.

Join the jolly jellyfish!

Look out for the magic dragon!

Watch out!   Whirlpools!

There's a wizard in Shark Castle!

Pirates ahoy!

What is in the Floating Forest?

35

Monster Magic

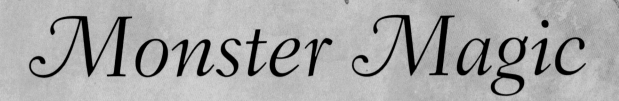

*S*omeone who loved Kerry very much kissed her good night and gave her a hug. Kerry held on tight. "Don't go!" she whispered.

At first Kerry didn't want to tell why she was scared. At last, she said in a very, very quiet voice:

"There's a monster in my wardrobe."

The grown-up who so much wanted Kerry to be happy looked serious. "I'm glad you told me, Kerry. Don't worry. I can deal with this. You stay right where you are."

Kerry pulled her quilt right up to her eyes and peered over the top. The grown-up marched over to the wardrobe, gently opened the door, had a good look inside, and shut it again.

"Is it there?" asked Kerry.

The grown-up who loved Kerry every minute of every day nodded. "It's worse than you thought. Not one monster but four! A mother and her children."

Kerry gulped. The grown-up came over and sat down. "Now Kerry, I will tell the monsters to go, but I'm going to have to ask you to shut your eyes. You see, well, don't laugh, but *they don't have any clothes on*. They feel embarrassed."

Kerry tried hard not to giggle. She shut her eyes tight. There was the sound of a wardrobe door opening. "Leave now, and quickly please. And don't ever come back!"

After a few minutes, Kerry opened her eyes. The grown-up gave her a thumbs-up sign. "We did it!"

*Just why monsters take their clothes off in wardrobes I really don't know. They do it under beds, too, sometimes. You might want to mention that to your grown-up if you ever have a problem like Kerry's. And please **try** not to laugh!*

New Friends

When Dad picked Jilly up from school, she was sitting by herself and looking sad. She was very quiet in the car, too.

"Now, Jilly-Jilly-Jelly-Welly," Dad smiled. "You know as well as I do that the best thing to do is to tell your old dad all about whatever is upsetting you."

Jilly sighed. "Mandie wouldn't play with me today," she said. "There was a new girl called Ella. Mandie stayed with her and they spent the whole day giggling."

Dad sighed, too. "Poor Mandie," he said.

"Poor Mandie?" yelled Jilly. "Poor Mandie?"

"Yes, poor Mandie. She didn't get to play with the best girl in the school today," said Dad. "Why didn't you play with your other friends?"

"I don't have any other friends, not really. I always play with Mandie."

"Then this is a great chance," said Dad. "There are lots of kids just waiting to play with you. Just think of all the friends you've missed making. All you have to do is smile and say hello."

"Will they really want to be friends with me?" asked Jilly quietly.

"They will if you really want to be friends with them," said Dad.

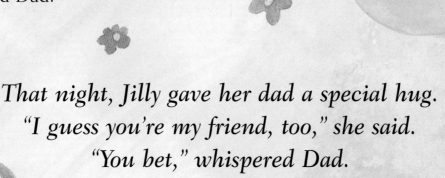

That night, Jilly gave her dad a special hug.
"I guess you're my friend, too," she said.
"You bet," whispered Dad.

Bouncy Bunny

Once upon a time, there was a little rabbit who would not keep still. All rabbits are a little bit bouncy, but this one went bounce…

boing!

bounce!

boing!

all day long.

One night, the little rabbit's granny came to bunnysit.

"This bouncing is fine in the daytime," she said firmly. "You feel as if you have springs in your knees and your feet and your paws. But I want you to imagine those springs turning into … spaghetti! Then you will be

floppy…

and flippy…

and sloppy…

and slippy…

and flollop right into your bed."

And the little rabbit was so floppy and flollopy that he fell fast asleep. (And so did Granny!)

*What happens to **your** springs if they turn into spaghetti? Just try it!*

41

Funny Faces

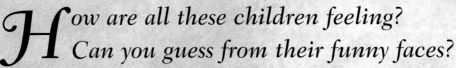

How are all these children feeling?
Can you guess from their funny faces?

I am angry. Very angry. Very angry indeed!

I am really happy. I want to dance and sing!

I am so, so tired!

I am really worried about something.

I am feeling very sad.

I am excited about what will happen tomorrow!

42

I am bored.

I am sorry I made some bad choices today.

I feel warm and safe and snuggly.

I am feeling wide awake!

I am missing someone I love.

I am feeling quiet and calm.

How are you feeling tonight?
Can you tell your special grown-up all about it?
It is good to share your feelings with someone
you love ... whatever they are.

Little Angel

One night, when Sophie was staying with her grandma, she said that she was scared to go to sleep.

"Oh, sweetheart, you don't need to be afraid," said Grandma. "Don't you know that you have a guardian angel looking after you *all* the time?"

"What's a guardian angel?" asked Sophie.

"It's someone very special, who always cares about you," said Grandma. "You can't see her, but she watches over you all the time so that you are safe."

Sophie felt happy as she went to sleep. When she was back at home, she told her best friend Ellie all about it.

Ellie frowned. "My dad says angels are just made up," she said. "There isn't really anyone watching over you."

Sophie was upset. That night, she told her mother she was frightened to go to sleep. "You see, there aren't really any angels," she said.

Her mother gave her a hug. "I don't know if you have a guardian angel," she said, "but I do know that every minute of every day and every night you are loved by so, so many people, and cared about by so, so many people, and watched over by so, so many people. And you are safe all day and all night because so many people love you."

Sophie smiled and closed her eyes. Her mother kissed her and whispered, "And as for angels. I know they are real because I have one *right here*."

Think about all the people who love you as you go to sleep. They think YOU are an angel, too.

45

Always There

Whenever Keisha went out with her mother, she looked up at Mrs. Asa's window. Mrs. Asa lived next door. She was always there, waving and smiling. It was the same when they came home. Mrs. Asa was always there.

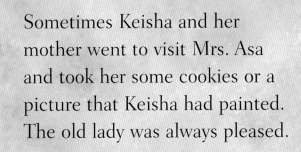

Sometimes Keisha and her mother went to visit Mrs. Asa and took her some cookies or a picture that Keisha had painted. The old lady was always pleased.

"It makes my day to see your little beaming face," she told Keisha, giving her a hug.

One day, Keisha's mother told her, "I don't want you to worry, sweetheart, but Mrs. Asa was taken to the hospital last night. She hasn't been feeling well for a while."

Now when Keisha went out or came home, Mrs. Asa's window looked very empty. "I can't wait for her to come back," said Keisha.

But a week later, Keisha's mother held her hand and told her that Mrs. Asa wouldn't be coming back. "She was very, very old, and she has died," said her mother. "It means that we won't see her at her window any more. It is sad for us, but she is all right now and won't ever feel tired or ill again."

"But she was always there!" cried Keisha.

"Now she is somewhere else," said her mother.

"Where?"

"Here," said Keisha's mother, gently touching the little girl's chest. "Here in your heart and here," she went on, stroking Keisha's head, "in your memories. Mrs. Asa is always there, and she always will be if you think about her now and then."

People and places and happy times don't ever really leave us, if we keep them safe inside. They are always there for us.

Future Friends

One night, Zoe told her dad that she didn't ever, *ever*, EVER want to go to preschool again.

"I thought you had fun with your friends there," said Dad.

"That was before Martin came," Zoe muttered. "He's mean and horrible. He isn't ever going to be my friend."

"Tell me all about him," Dad replied.

So Zoe told Dad about all the mean things that Martin had done to her and her friends. It did sound pretty bad. He had taken their toys, and said unkind things, and even pushed and pinched and pulled Katie's hair.

Dad was quiet for a moment. "You have all had a sad time," he said, "and I mean Martin, too. He must be a very unhappy boy to do all those things. I think we should ask him to play."

"I don't really want to," said Zoe with a frown.

"Trust me," said Dad. "I'll be there, and I would never let anyone be mean to you."

The next day, Martin and his mother came home with Zoe and her dad after preschool. While the grown-ups chatted, the children played happily together.

That night, Zoe's dad told her, "I was really proud of you today. You played so well with Martin, although you didn't want to."

"He's OK when you get to know him," Zoe admitted.

"He had a hard time before he came here, and he was scared," Dad explained. "What he did wasn't good, and you were right to tell me all about it. Do you still think you can never be friends?"

"We're already friends," said Zoe. "Thanks, Dad."

At Home

Once there was a little bird who lived with his mother and father in a snug nest under the eaves of an old barn.

"Time to wiggle those wings, William," said his father one day. "Tomorrow we will set off for our winter home. It's a long way to Africa, but we'll be with you every flap of the way."

"What do you mean 'our winter home'?" asked William. "This is my home right here. I don't want to go anywhere."

"Soon it will be cold here," his mother explained. "We have a lovely warm place in Africa. Don't worry. We'll come back here in the spring."

The little family was soon ready to set off. Lots of their friends were making the same journey. The next morning, as the sun rose over the fields, the birds rose up together and soared into the sky. All except one…

William hid behind the barn and watched as the others disappeared into the sky. Then he flew back to his old nest and settled down. "Ah, there's no place like home," he chirrupped.

But as the day passed, William began to feel lonely. Somehow his home didn't seem so snug with just one little bird in it.

Long before the sun went down, there was a fluttering above the nest. William's parents had come back to find him.

"We know you love your home," they said. "But you do need to come with us."

William didn't even begin to argue. "I'll come," he agreed. "I know that home isn't here or there, it's wherever we are. All of us together."

51

Moon Music

In the soft, dark night, Moon was twirling slowly high in the sky. She looked down at the Earth below and saw all kinds of things.

"That is the way the world is," smiled Moon.
"Things are changing all the time."

What changes are happening to you?
Whatever they are, one thing doesn't change.
You are a very special person,
and you always will be.

53

Just Me

One day, Ian went to play with his friend Marla. Her house was the busiest, noisiest, funniest place that Ian had ever been. You see, Marla had **six** brothers and sisters!

As he walked home that night, Ian was very quiet. His mother asked him if he would like to tell her what the trouble was.

"Not really," said Ian. "I don't want to upset you."

"Upset me?" Ian's mother gave him a hug and a big smile. "That's kind, sweetheart, but you know, the thing about grown-ups is that they can look after themselves. You don't need to worry about *me*. Now, tell me about *you*."

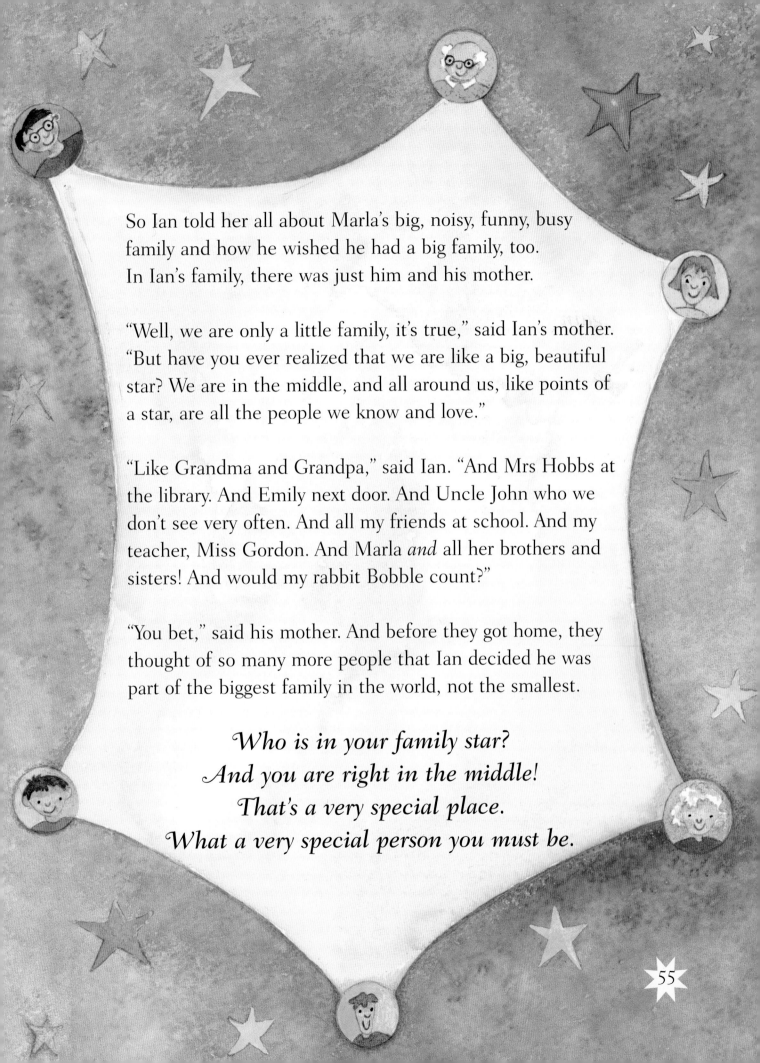

So Ian told her all about Marla's big, noisy, funny, busy family and how he wished he had a big family, too. In Ian's family, there was just him and his mother.

"Well, we are only a little family, it's true," said Ian's mother. "But have you ever realized that we are like a big, beautiful star? We are in the middle, and all around us, like points of a star, are all the people we know and love."

"Like Grandma and Grandpa," said Ian. "And Mrs Hobbs at the library. And Emily next door. And Uncle John who we don't see very often. And all my friends at school. And my teacher, Miss Gordon. And Marla *and* all her brothers and sisters! And would my rabbit Bobble count?"

"You bet," said his mother. And before they got home, they thought of so many more people that Ian decided he was part of the biggest family in the world, not the smallest.

Who is in your family star?
And you are right in the middle!
That's a very special place.
What a very special person you must be.

The Hugaluga

Zip! Zap! A quick little fish flashed past Mariella the mermaid just as she was drifting off to sleep. Zoom! Zip! There he was again! Mariella sat up and frowned.

"Little Fish!" she said. "It is bedtime. Find yourself a nice wavy weed and go to sleep!"

But the little fish would not keep still. "I'm not tired," he said. "Not a bit! And I love to zap and zoom and zip!"

"You've been zapping and zooming and zipping all day," Mariella replied. "Your quick little body needs to rest."

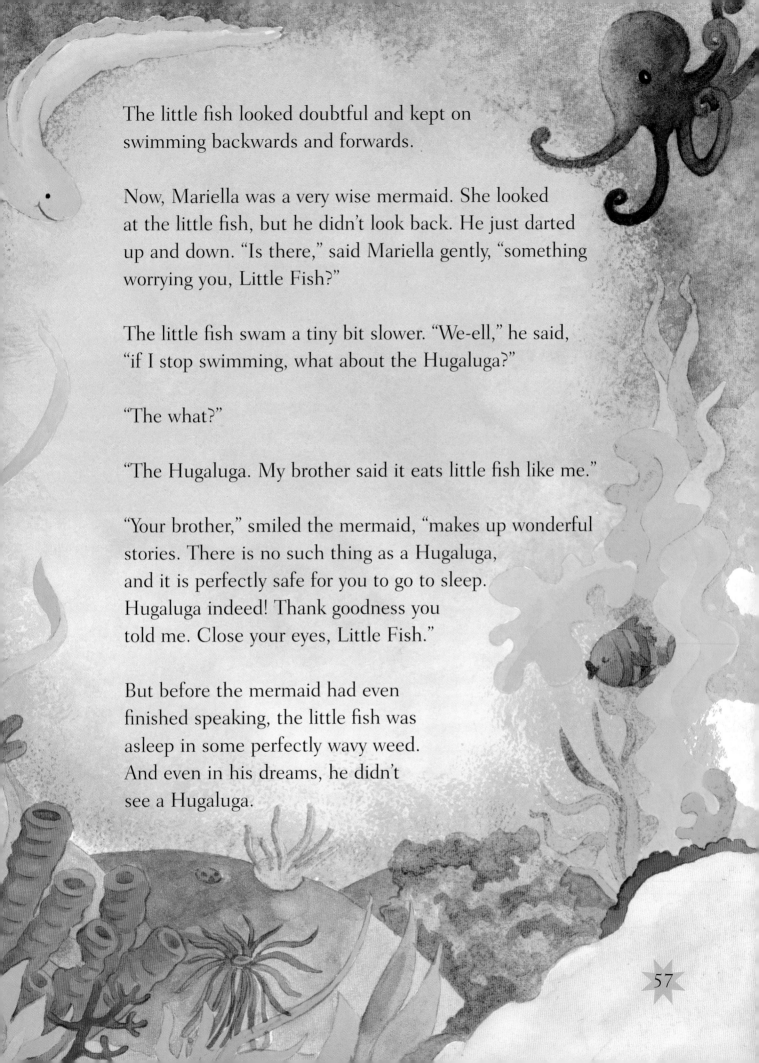

The little fish looked doubtful and kept on swimming backwards and forwards.

Now, Mariella was a very wise mermaid. She looked at the little fish, but he didn't look back. He just darted up and down. "Is there," said Mariella gently, "something worrying you, Little Fish?"

The little fish swam a tiny bit slower. "We-ell," he said, "if I stop swimming, what about the Hugaluga?"

"The what?"

"The Hugaluga. My brother said it eats little fish like me."

"Your brother," smiled the mermaid, "makes up wonderful stories. There is no such thing as a Hugaluga, and it is perfectly safe for you to go to sleep. Hugaluga indeed! Thank goodness you told me. Close your eyes, Little Fish."

But before the mermaid had even finished speaking, the little fish was asleep in some perfectly wavy weed. And even in his dreams, he didn't see a Hugaluga.

Bad Bob Bear

When Billy Bear was angry, he stamped his feet, and growled, and threw things, and even cried sometimes.

Grandpa Bear sat down to tell Billy a story.

"I'm not listening!" said Billy.

"Never mind," said Grandpa, "I'll tell it to myself. Ahem! Once upon a time, there was a bear called Bad Bob Bear. At least, that's how he felt sometimes. He seemed to have great big feelings inside that he just couldn't manage."

"So? I don't care," said Billy rudely.

"Well," said Grandpa, "one day Bad Bob Bear's Grampy (that's what he called his grandpa) said to him, 'You know, when you're quiet and happy, I love you a lot. But when you have great big feelings that frighten you, I love you just as much.'"

Billy Bear turned. "How could he?"

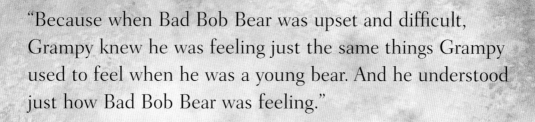

"Because when Bad Bob Bear was upset and difficult, Grampy knew he was feeling just the same things Grampy used to feel when he was a young bear. And he understood just how Bad Bob Bear was feeling."

"Do you? Did he? Does he? Did you?" cried Billy.

"You're not alone, Billy Bear," said the old bear. "We've all had big feelings. Come and tell me about it. I'll still love you no matter what it is."

"Really?" asked Billy. He felt better already.

"Really," said Grandpa. "My Grampy told me that, and now I'm telling you."

"You mean *you're* Bad Bob Bear?" said Billy.

"I never was, really," smiled Grandpa. "I was just Bob Bear who needed a friend. And you're not Bad Billy Bear, either."

"Because I do have a friend," sighed Billy as he snuggled up to Grandpa for a bedtime chat.

Someone Special

Here is a rhyme to read to any child. Simply change "he" or "she" to suit your child and choose one of the alternative endings if you are reading to more than one child.

The world is full of children
And most of them are fun
But every single parent
Wants a really *special* one.

She may be big, she may be small,
When all is said and done,
The only thing that matters is
That she's a *special* one.

A child may like to sit and think,
A child may love to run,
But what's really most important
Is that he's a *special* one.

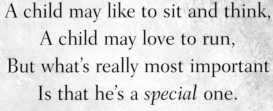

If a little child does naughty things,
(Most children do, I find,)
Everything will be forgiven
If she is the *special* kind.

In our family we are lucky
Because we always knew
We had a very special child
As soon as we saw *you!*

Alternative endings:
We don't have just *one* special child
We have a special *two!*

We don't have just *one* special child
We have *you* and *you* and *you!*

Near and Far

Honey went to sleep every night in her own snuggly bed. She felt safe and warm from the tips of her toes to the top of her head. And every night, someone very special to her said good night and tickled those toes and kissed the very top of that little head.

One night, the someone very special said, "I have to go away for a few days, sweetheart. You are going to stay with Aunty Lynn. Won't that be fun? What a grown-up girl you will be!"

Honey agreed that it was exciting. She was very happy to help the someone very special to pack her own little bag. She chose which cuddly toy to take with her. She made sure that the storybook she loved best was packed as well.

When Honey arrived at Aunty Lynn's house, she was met with a huge hug. Honey's special someone smiled. "You're going to have such a good time, Honey. I'll see you on Friday."

Honey did have a good time. She had spaghetti and ice cream for supper. She took a big, bubbly bath, and the water was pink! Aunty Lynn had huge, fluffy towels and a special way of brushing her hair without pulling *at all*.

But when Honey was sitting up in her bed, she suddenly felt a little bit sad. Aunty Lynn didn't know about tickling her toes and kissing the very top of her head.

Then Aunty Lynn gave Honey a funny striped hat that her special someone often wore. It even smelled a little bit like that missing person. "Friday isn't far away," she said.

Honey went to sleep wearing the hat. She knew she looked funny, but it was like having a kiss on the top of her head all night. Aunty Lynn was right. Friday really wasn't far away.

Friendly Fish

Harrison was a tiny yellow fish in a huge ocean. Sometimes he felt lonely.

"Why don't you go and play with all those little fish swimming over there?" his mother suggested.

Harrison swam eagerly over. He wiggled his fins in a way that means (in fish language) "Can I play with you, please?"

At once, the school of little fish wiggled back and swam straight at Harrison. He swished away as fast as he could and hid behind his mother's rock.

"They won't let me play," he told her. "They chased me away." He spent the rest of the day hiding.

Harrison felt lonelier than ever. "You should try again," said his father. "I'm sure those are friendly fish."

But again, when Harrison went near, the fish turned and swam straight at him.

That night, Harrison had a long talk with his mother. "You must tell those other fish how you feel," she said. "Maybe they don't understand."

In the morning, Harrison went right up to the school of little fish. "Sometimes I feel lonely," he said. "I would love to play with you. It makes me sad when you chase me away."

"Chase you away? We're playing 'tag' with you!" burbled the fish. "Of course we want to play!" And they swam straight at Harrison.

This time Harrison swam away as fast as before, but there was a smile on his fishy face.

It's easy for there to be misunderstandings between friends. Talking about it is best!

Birthday Boy

Nathan was so excited about his birthday that he didn't know what to do. His insides were feeling wiggly and jiggly. He felt like laughing one minute and crying the next.

"You need something to take your mind off tomorrow," said dad. "Why don't you watch that movie you love so much?"

Nathan watched seventeen minutes of his movie before the wiggly, jiggly feeling came back.

He went upstairs and came down ... dressed for bed!

"Hey, what are you doing?" cried his dad. "It's half-past three in the afternoon!"

"I thought if I went to bed, tomorrow would come more quickly," Nathan explained.

"I doubt it," said Dad, "but you can try it if you like."

So Nathan went up to bed. But that wiggly, jiggly feeling inside was still there. Nathan trailed downstairs.

"I've got another idea," he told his dad. Dad groaned.

"What if we have my birthday *today*?" Nathan grinned. "Then I won't have to wait."

"Nice try, Nate," replied Dad. "Come on, let's go out."

Dad took Nathan to the park. They ran, and climbed, and swung, and rolled down the slope. Then they went to the indoor play place. They jumped, and roller-skated, and ate ice cream.

"Now we're going to run all the way home," said Dad.

Nathan's mother came home at half-past six. "Are you a very excited birthday boy?" she called from the front door. But there was no answer from Nathan. (And there was no answer from Dad either!)

Tiger Trouble

When Dad came home with a new tent, Ashley and Lewis whooped and jumped up and down.

"Get off the sofa!" shouted Dad. "And give me a hand with all this." He seemed to have bought a lot in the camping store.

The next weekend, they drove out to the woods. "Why is it taking so long?" asked the boys, looking at Dad's red face as he struggled with the tent.

At last the tent was up. "This is the life!" said Dad, beaming at the boys as he burned the sausages.

It was dark when Ashley and Lewis crawled into the tent. Dad was tidying up. Lewis snuggled into his sleeping bag and shut his eyes. Ashley went to sleep right away.

Lewis stared at the dark. Outside, he could hear rustling sounds. He was even sure he could hear breathing and growling. There were tigers outside. He knew it! Then came the noise of the tent flap opening. The tigers were coming!

Lewis grabbed his flashlight. It was a big, heavy one. As a dark shape moved slowly towards him, he lifted it up and thwacked the shape as hard as he could.

"Owwwwwwww!" howled the tiger. Only it was a tiger who sounded a lot like Dad!

When Dad's head stopped hurting, and Ashley had gone to sleep once more, Dad gave Lewis a hug. "Brave boy," he whispered, "I'm not much good at putting up tents, and I'm no genius at cooking sausages, but I am an *expert* dad. And I would never let *anything*, not even tigers, hurt you."

Lewis smiled and closed his eyes. He knew that was true.

I know you have someone special who keeps you safe, even from tigers. Isn't that a good feeling?

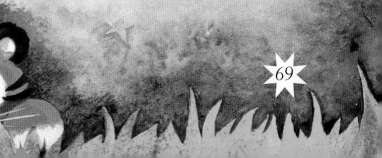

69

Fred's Bedroom

There was a little bear called Fred
Who didn't want to go to bed.
He stamped his paws and shook his head.
"I just don't like my room," he said.

"Don't like your room?" said Mother Bear.
"My furry Fred, are you aware
That at your age, I had to share
With *all* my sisters? Was that fair?"

Growled Grandpa, "Fair? You should be told
Of times when bears were brave and bold.
There were no rooms in days of old.
We had a cave—dark, damp, and cold."

Great-Grandma waved her furry paws.
"My story is much worse than yours.
We had no roof, or walls, or floors.
All through the year we lived outdoors!"

There was no sound from little Fred.
He thought of all that had been said
And up the stairs he quickly fled
To his own room, and his own bed.

Counting Sheep

*S*ome people say that if you have trouble
getting to sleep, you should count sheep!
Try this funny rhyme to see if it's true!

Ten little sheep were feeling fine,
One ran away, and then there were nine.

Nine little sheep were going through the gate,
One stayed behind, and then there were eight.

Eight little sheep thought buttercups were heaven.
One had to stop and rest, and then there were seven.

Seven little sheep were getting in a fix,
One tumbled in the mud, and then there were six.

Six little sheep were looking at a hive,
One got stung right on his nose, and then there were five!

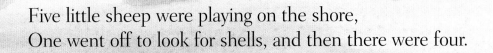

Five little sheep were playing on the shore,
One went off to look for shells, and then there were four.

Four little sheep decided to go to sea,
One hopped onto an island, and then there were three.

Three little sheep didn't know just what to do,
One decided to swim to shore, and then there were two.

Two little sheep floated off towards the sun.
One went to sleep in the bottom of the boat, and then there was one.

Away sailed the little boat and one little sheep.
They drifted into dreamland. It's time for you to sleep...

It's Not Fair!

*J*ack didn't think it was fair that he had to go to bed before his big sister. When it was time for bed, he always complained.

"Jack, we've been over and over this," said his dad. "Ella is two years older than you. She always has been and she always will be. And that means that she is a big girl and goes to bed just a little bit later."

"You bet," said Ella, which just made Jack wail louder.

"It's not fair!" he yelled. "Why can't I stay up longer?"

But Dad had picked Jack up and whisked him upstairs before he had even finished half a wail.

Jack went right on wailing while Dad helped him get ready for bed.

Several times, while Jack yelled,
Dad shut his eyes for a moment
and seemed to be counting.

At last Jack was ready to be put
into his own little bed.

"You know what's really silly about this,
Jack?" said his dad. "I know, and you know, that you are so
tired you need to fall asleep right now! But just because
Ella is still up, you don't want to. I think you're worried that
you're being left out, and something great is happening
downstairs that you are missing. Am I right?"

Jack stopped wailing and stared. "Let me tell you," said
Dad, "nothing exciting is happening. Ella is going on and on
about wanting a rabbit. You know she does that all the time.
Your mother is paying some bills and I, in a minute, will be
watching the news. Does any of that sound exciting?"

Well, no, it didn't. Jack felt glad to be in his snuggly bed.
He fell asleep before Dad had tiptoed out of the room.

What happens downstairs when you go to bed?
Is it anywhere near as exciting as the dreams
you are going to have ... right now?

Beds Everywhere!

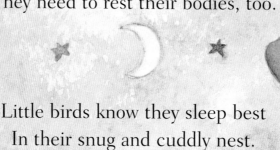

Living things are just like you.
They need to rest their bodies, too.

Little birds know they sleep best
In their snug and cuddly nest.

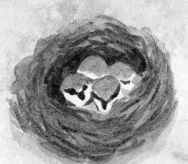

A kitten, after hours of fun,
Curls up in her basket when day is done.

Bouncy bunnies can be found
Snug and asleep beneath the ground.

Puppies like to run and play,
But find their bed at the end of the day.

A baby elephant shuts his eyes
Under wide and starry skies.

A little mouse will quickly creep
Into his hole to fall asleep.

A tired frog is very fond
Of his weedy bed beside the pond.

Little fishes sleep and dream
Under the rocks of their moonlit stream.

Even flowers nod their heads
And fall asleep in their garden beds.

And what do little people do?
They need a place for dreaming, too.
The very best place for your sleepy head
Is safe and warm in your own little bed.

Rocked Asleep

Some things change, and some things stay the same, but bedtime is always a special time...

At night in the nursery, before she went to bed, Charlotte rode on Starlight, her beautiful rocking horse. Then she hugged him, whispered something special in his ear, and climbed into bed. And as Charlotte slept, Starlight gently rocked and brought her peaceful dreams.

Well, Charlotte grew up and had a little girl of her own. In Ruby's bedroom stood her beautiful rocking horse. Guess what he was called! Yes, Starlight. Before she went to bed, Ruby hugged him, and whispered something special in his ear. As Ruby slept, Starlight gently rocked and brought her peaceful dreams.

Well, Ruby grew up, too. Soon she had a little boy of her own. He was called Richard. In Richard's room, his beautiful rocking horse was waiting each evening. Richard hugged him, and whispered something special in his ear. And as Richard slept, Starlight gently rocked and brought him peaceful dreams.

Yes, you are right. Richard grew up and became a dad. His little twins loved Starlight just as much as he did. At night, they hugged him, and whispered something special into *both* his ears, and clambered into bed. And as they slept, Starlight gently rocked and brought them peaceful dreams.

If you had a rocking horse called Starlight,
what would you whisper in his ear?
Who could you whisper to instead?
Sweet dreams!

Choosing a Story